TENTACLE SUBMISSION

RILEY ROSE

BOOK TWO IN THE TANTALIZING TENTACLES SERIES

A STORY IN THE DECADENT FANTASY UNIVERSE

CHAPTER ONE

My eyes fluttered open to the gentle rocking of the boat and the feel of a soft, slimy tentacle working its way up my leg. Normally that would be a great reason to freak out. But I merely relaxed against its soothing touch.

The tentacle belonged to Kez, a very unique creature I discovered in a cave near Barbados that Blackbeard had used to store his treasure.

I had helped free Kez from the cave and he had fucked me in ways I didn't know were possible with his many sensual tendrils. And then he asked me to be his girlfriend. I know, it's weird. But he's actually really sweet and no one can make me a submissive slut like he can.

So we've been navigating the Atlantic the past couple of weeks, having fun and cumming more than I have in my entire life.

"Mmm, Kez," I murmured. "It's too early to get up."

My many-armed lover caressed both my legs, tugging on me gently.

"C'mon, just five more minutes, okay?"

Kez was having none of that.

I yelped as he grabbed my ankle and yanked me out of bed.

I flew through the cabin and out the door, where he held me upside down over the deck.

My T-shirt fell and covered my face, revealing my skimpy lavender panties and huge bare tits, my nipples immediately hardening in the cool morning air.

"Kez!" I tried to yell through my shirt. I couldn't see anything with it covering my face and getting tangled in my arms.

He lifted me up and down by my foot, making my juicy tits bounce sexily. Then he tickled my sides with a couple of his smaller tendrils.

"Kez... will... you... knock it off?" I said between giggling fits. Why did I have to find such a mischievous tentacle boyfriend?

I finally got my shirt off and let it drop to the deck. I saw several of Kez's tentacles on the deck. His main, large body was next to my yacht, underwater. That's where he was most comfortable, but it definitely didn't stop him from getting plenty of his arms on the ship to have fun with me.

I dangled there, his tendrils moving all over me and continuing to make my boobs jiggle.

"You're really enjoying yourself, aren't you?"

I knew he was laughing down in the water, or whatever the equivalent of laughing was for his species.

He whisked me off the anchored boat and dunked me in the water.

"Ahh!" I screamed when he pulled me out. "Kez, that's really cold!"

He dunked me again, and this time I could see his kind-of-squid/kind-of-octopus/kind-of-not-either body. Yup, he was definitely laughing.

I sputtered water when he brought me out a second time and then raised me back over the deck, still holding me upside down.

He yanked my soaked panties off and grabbed a bunch of towels from inside the cabin, drying me off like a car wash.

When I was nice and dry, he deposited me on a lounge chair on the deck and wrapped me up in his tentacles. I could feel warmth emanating from them, immediately taking all the chill away. See, told you he was sweet.

He slid a large tendril between my legs and entered me.

I gasped as my tight pussy was filled with his manhood, well, tentacle-hood.

I felt him in my mind. That was the way we communicated. Whenever he was inside me, I could sense what he was saying.

"Well, good morning to you too." I smiled and caressed his tendrils. Yes, it was a rude awakening, but I couldn't really be mad, especially with how much love I was sensing from him.

He lifted a medium-sized tentacle to my mouth, and I let him slip it inside. He felt warm and sweet as I twirled my tongue around him and we made out. He was a really good kisser.

He worked his big boy farther into my pussy, making me groan into the tentacle he had in my mouth. The more he filled me, the better I could sense his thoughts.

He thought my light brown skin looked beautiful glistening in the morning sun.

"Aw, Kez, you're such a sweetheart."

He gave me a nice, gentle morning fucking, working his huge cock in and out of my tight cavern.

"Ohh Kez, that feels so good."

He tied my hands above me to the chaise lounge and fondled my huge tits. He knew how much it turned me on when he tied me up.

I sucked on the tentacle he had in my mouth. His slippery manhood tasted salty-sweet and I closed my eyes as I took even more of him.

I moaned softly as he filled me all the way to my cervix and expanded my pussy walls as far as possible.

My moans increased as he slowly increased his fucking speed. I sucked him harder, wanting him to jizz in my mouth at the same time he forced me to expel my sweet girl juices.

My pussy squeezed his huge cock tightly as he plundered it in only the way he could. He squeezed my tits tighter and tugged on my nipples as he felt my orgasm coming.

He thrust extremely hard into me. My groans would have been audible if not for his cock in my mouth.

I came hard, my nectar spilling out around his huge member. He pulled out of me and attacked my clit, so I could freely squirt my cum all over the place. He really loved seeing me spray my sauce.

He also loved my slutty screams, so he removed the smaller tendril in my mouth, and I let loose.

"Ohhhhhhhhuhhhhhhhhh!

He squeezed my clit so hard, spurt after spurt of cum came flying out of my pussy.

Then he rammed both cocks back into me and came into my pussy and mouth simultaneously.

I squirmed as huge blasts of his cum filled my pussy. I greedily drank up his seed. It tasted like a sweeter form of milk, and I had discovered it also provided nourishment.

He shot a couple more spurts into my pussy and then whipped both tentacles out of me, giving me a nice present as he came over my stomach and tits.

"Oh, geez, Kez, you really know how to make me your slut."

He slipped back inside me so he could communicate that my statement was very accurate.

"Okay, well, let me go take a shower, so I can get your tasty juice off me and wake up more fully."

He thought the fucking he just gave me was an excellent wake-up call.

"Okay, yes, it definitely was. But I still need to shower."

He unbound me and joined me in the tiny shower. I could barely move with his tentacles in there with me. He took it upon himself to wash my hair and body. He spent a lot of time in particular washing my tits, pussy, and ass.

I laughed. "Okay, Kez, I think I'm clean."

After helping me dry off again, I rifled through my clothing options.

Kez pointed to the skimpiest swimsuit I had. A yellow thong that showed off virtually all of my firm, juicy ass and a very small bikini top. I had actually bought it just for Kez. I figured it would turn him on and apparently I was right.

"Of course you want that one."

He picked the two pieces up and handed them to me.

"Okay, okay."

I pulled the thong on, feeling the soft fabric slip between my ass cheeks. Then put the top on, letting Kez tie it behind my back. He was very dexterous, especially with his smaller tendrils.

"How do I look?"

Whack! He answered with a sultry slap on my ass.

I grinned. "Okay, guess you really like it."

I put the ship on auto-pilot. Then puttered over to the kitchenette and fixed myself a light breakfast, since Kez's secret sauce provided plenty of nutrients.

Kez busied himself eating fish, crabs, and whatever else he ate while I munched on French toast and fruit.

When I was finished, his tentacles scooped me up, bent me over the table, pulled my thong aside, and fucked the shit out of me.

I lay on the table and panted after he was done filling me with his jizz and draining me of my juices.

"Damn Kez... you're... really horny today."

He slapped me on my ass, letting me know I was right.

I was considering asking him to go another round when I heard screaming.

I rushed up on deck and to the bow. The shore was in sight. It was so early the light was still faint and we were too far away for me to make much out. But I could tell there were a few figures on the docks and I definitely heard the very loud screams and shouts of two distinct female voices.

Shit!

"Kez let's go," I yelled as I scrambled into the wheelhouse and threw the throttle full ahead.

Time to save the day.

CHAPTER TWO

So I initially thought the two women were being attacked. As we got closer, I realized that was definitely not the case.

They were being fucked. Hard. And from the sounds of things were really enjoying it.

"Oh my God he's so big!" a sultry voice moaned.

"Ram it in my tight little pussy!" a higher, younger voice cried out.

"Make us take every inch of your delicious zombie cocks!" the first voice screamed submissively.

Zombie what? I wasn't sure what exactly was going on over there - maybe it was a costume party or something and some guys were dressed as zombies. Whatever it was, it was turning me on like crazy. I could feel my crotch moisten at the continued moans and screams from the two sexy sounding ladies.

I knew I probably shouldn't, but I really wanted to get a closer look at this crazy fuckfest that was going on. And hopefully see some incredibly hot naked bodies.

Kez's tendrils softly wrapped around me as I stood thinking about it. I had become very used to it. He loved being in contact with my body, and I found it very relaxing.

I pulled the front of my thong out and he immediately

slipped inside it and entered me. Even though he had done that like a million times the past two weeks, he still made me gasp every time. Fuck he really filled me to perfection.

"So Kez, what say we sneak up closer and get a look at these kinky sexpots?"

I felt him pulse inside my center as he sent me a question.

"Will it make me even hornier and make me want you to completely dominate me? Um, yeah there's an extremely high likelihood of that happening."

Another pussy pulse. He was totally okay with it.

"Great. Let's go be sneaky peepers."

I navigated the boat closer as Kez swam beside it. And still stayed inside my pussy. Honestly he spent so much time inside me, he might as well list it as his permanent address.

As we approached the dock, the sultry screams got louder and more intense. Apparently the two women were being fucked even harder. I felt Kez worm farther into me, making me groan. He must have been getting turned on just as much as I was.

"I know, right?" I said to him. "These chicks are some super-sexy sluts."

He made a quippy reply. I made a face at him.

"Yes, I realize I am a huge slut for you all the time. Why do you think I'm so turned on by them?"

I stuck my tongue out playfully. "Now shush while I get us nice and close to see some hot asses."

The dawn haze let us creep up really close to the dock, the yacht silently cutting through the water as I cut the engines. Of course, the way they were going at it, they might not have noticed us no matter how loud the boat was.

I dashed back out to the bow, not bothering to drop the anchor. I knew Kez could keep the ship in place in the gentle water.

As I reached the railing by the prow, I got a very good view of the sexy shenanigans.

I focused on the two women first. They were both incredibly sexy. One was in her mid-20s, had an exotic face that looked like a mix of Asian and European, and sported short dark brown hair and an amazingly toned body. The other was a little younger with a cute American girl-next-door look and a light brown ponytail - not as athletic as her female fuck buddy but still very sensual with a shapely body and ridiculously juicy tits.

Seeing both of the naked women was making me very wet. As was the position they were in - they were standing, pressed against each other, their tits smashed together as they were bent forward and fucked from behind by their partners.

And as my eyes moved to the guys fucking them, that's when things got really weird.

They were zombies.

Like real, actual zombies.

What the fuck?!

I mean unless I just stumbled onto a horror film shoot, these two sexy sirens were being fucked by actual zombies. And were loving it.

"Uhhhh, fuck, make us your zombie sluts!" the super-athletic one shouted.

"We need your creepy undead jizz so bad!" her cute friend added.

Holy shit. This was so fucking weird.

Of course, I really shouldn't talk. My boyfriend was an unknown creature that fucked me ridiculously hard with his huge tentacles all day and night. But Kez's tentacles were so cute. Zombies just seemed, well, gross.

However, I still couldn't look away. It was crazy hot. Mainly because how into it the two beautiful women were.

Their lips were smashed together and they kissed each other passionately as the zombies rammed their huge, undead cocks ridiculously hard into both of their tight pussies. Okay, I really didn't know if they were tight, but I bet they were. I mean the zombie's huge cocks must have felt crazy tight inside them. I knew that feeling well.

On cue, Kez slunk his big cock-arm up the side of the boat, pulled my thong down just enough, and plunged into my very ready pussy. He immediately went all the way into me until he touched my cervix.

"Holy fuck Kez!" I tried to scream quietly to not alert the people, well two people and two zombies, on shore that we were there. They didn't seem to notice. Well, they were a little preoccupied.

Kez started fucking me very hard. I think he wanted to outdo the zombies. I grasped the railing to stay on my feet as my legs buckled from the savage thrusting.

I glanced back toward the shore and saw the zombies had pinned both women's arms behind their backs as they continued to dominate them. Guess zombies liked it kinky too.

The zombies grabbed the hair of both sexy sluts and yanked their heads back. Okay, this was getting hotter and hotter.

The women couldn't quite reach each others' lips anymore so they stuck their tongues out and let them dance together.

Meanwhile, Kez had thought up ways to turn me into an even bigger slut than the super-submissive women I was ogling.

He pulled me onto the railing so my feel and arms were dangling and my ass and pussy prominently displayed. Which allowed him to create even more fantastic sensations within my center as he expanded my pussy walls to near-bursting.

"Ohhhhh Kez... that... feels so good! But I can't see the

super-sexy naked ladies."

He tied my arms behind my back and yanked my head up by my long dark brown hair so I could see the zombie fuck-a-thon going on.

Both sexy women were screaming the sluttiest things I had ever heard and were moaning at the loudest decibels ever as their zombie lovers pummeled their dripping pussies.

I wasn't far behind them. Kez was completely having his way with me in the position he had put me in. My thong was around my thighs, my clit pressed against the cool metal railing, and my pussy being totally dominated by my favorite tentacle creature. It was almost overwhelming how much of him was inside me, but it was just shy of that too much pain threshold where I wanted nothing but for him to go harder and harder. Which he did, making me shriek louder and louder.

"Uhhhh… uhhhhhh… uhhhhhhhh… ohhhhhhhhhhh!"

My moans of desire mixed in with those of the very wet and naked women on the shore. Who were begging for the zombies to shoot their seed into them.

The undead sex machines were glad to oblige. I could see their bodies tense up and spasm, and I could tell from the women's reactions that a lot of zombie cum was flowing into them. I didn't know if that was gross or hot. Probably a little of both. But I was too busy being on the verge of my own orgasm and wanting Kez to do to me what those zombies did to their naked nymphs.

"Oh my fucking God Kez! Please shoot your sweet cum into me! I need it so bad!"

I groaned as his tentacle cock expanded briefly and then exploded with his cum.

"Ahhhhhhhhhhh!" I shrieked as my own orgasm crashed over me and I felt my slick juices spill out all over the railing.

I probably would have slipped right off it and fell into the cold water below if Kez wasn't holding me so tightly.

He pulled my long hair more firmly as he continued to thrust into me and give my pussy his sweet and salty gift.

I looked over at my two favorite zombie sluts and saw them fall to the wooden deck as their undead lovers pulled out of them and deposited more cum over their tits, stomachs and asses.

Which prompted Kez to yank his huge member out of me and shoot his jizz across my back and ass. Great. Now he was getting fucking tips from zombies. Except he knew it made me feel even sluttier and want him more.

He held me over the railing as mini-orgasms continued to detonate inside my core.

I watched the zombies stagger away from the two women, who were writhing on the ground, obviously still being consumed by their own post-orgasms.

I whimpered as my body continued to spasm and Kez stroked me affectionately. I noticed more zombies join their two pals. After what looked like a very brief zombie huddle, all of them shuffled back toward the two women. And this time they looked like they wanted to snack more than fuck.

The super-athletic sexpot immediately leapt to her feet, her juices still running down her amazingly sexy and tone legs. The younger one scrambled up and peeked out over the shoulder of her warrior friend.

They backed up slowly as the zombie horde advanced on them.

I flung my legs wildly. "Kez, get me down. We need to help them!"

He quickly put me back on my feet and yanked my thong back up as I bolted for the wheelhouse. I threw the throttle forward and the yacht rushed toward the dock.

The older woman grabbed two oars on the dock and tossed

one to her companion, while twirling hers expertly.

She whipped it around her, striking zombies in their gross heads and tripping them up. Wow. She was impressive. Seeing her kick ass while naked was definitely a sight to behold.

Her friend was not as skilled, but was trying her best. She bopped a zombie over the head multiple times with her oar but just looked like she was making it annoyed. However, her tits were jiggling very nicely as she attempted to fend it off. *Geez, Kione, focus. Ogle them more after you save them.*

I wasn't usually this obsessed with sex. Okay, maybe I was. Or maybe it was all the intense fucking Kez had been giving me.

I zipped the boat up to the dock way too fast. I tried to position the deck next to the wooden platform but wound up bumping against it.

The whole dock rocked, knocking the two women to the ground and a few zombies into the water.

Whoops. Well at least I took some of the undead lurchers out of the equation.

I stuck my head out the door. "Jump on!" I yelled to the women.

They didn't need to be asked twice. The kick-ass one leapt onto the deck and turned to catch her younger friend, who crashed into her, causing them both to sprawl onto the floor. In a rather erotic tangle of body parts.

Whoops. Obsessing about sex again. I dashed back behind the wheel and flung the throttle fully forward.

The zombies dove off the dock trying to get on board. The warrior chick scrambled up and kicked two of them over the railing, sending them splashing into the sea. The others fell into the water, not being able to cover the gap between the dock and the boat. So zombies were really bad at jumping.

And swimming. Good to know.

I set the auto-pilot on a heading out to sea, putting some distance between us and the zombies. Then hurried out to my super-hot, naked passengers.

"Are you guys okay?"

"We're good," the older woman said as she helped her companion up. "Thanks for the assist."

"Yeah perfect timing," her younger friend said perkily. Then she got a look at me.

"Holy shit! That's the skimpiest bikini I've ever seen."

"Casey!" the other woman admonished her.

"What? Oh c'mon Jess, I know you're getting wet looking at her."

I blushed, realizing just how little was covering me.

Jess shook her head. "What am I going to do with you?"

"Um, fuck my tight pussy a lot more?"

Jess laughed. "Well, okay, yes."

Casey looked back over at me. "Oh crap, I'm sorry, we're being rude. I'm Casey, this hot cum-covered slut is Jess."

Jess whacked Casey lightly. "Case! What the hell?"

"What?" her lover said innocently. "You're super-hot, have cum all over you, and don't pretend you don't love being a slut."

"Okay, you have just as much zombie juice on you and love being a slut too."

"True," Casey said agreeably. "But you ask me to tie you up and dominate you way more than I do."

Jess turned red, telling me her humorous girlfriend was right on the mark. Jess was obviously a girl after my own heart if she loved being bound and made to submit.

I smiled. "You two are cute." Then I hurried on, realizing that might have come out wrong. "I mean as a couple. Not that you're not both cute. I mean you're both really sexy. I mean…

I'm Kione."

I sighed. That was some nice word vomit.

Casey waved at me. "Oh what a beautiful name! For a sexy, beautiful lady. Who I see also has plenty of jizz on her. Where you just fucking a zombie too?"

"Casey!" Jess chastised her. "That's a little personal."

"Jess, we're standing here completely naked with cum all over us and Kione is nearly as naked and has almost as much cum on her. I don't know if we really need to worry about getting too personal."

Jess stuck her tongue out at her. "I hate it when you make sense."

Casey kissed her on the cheek. "Oh stop, you love it marshmallow."

"Marshmallow?" I asked.

Jess whacked her lover again. "Casey! That was supposed to be just between us."

"Oops. Well cat's out of the bag so I'll just tell her."

Jess rolled her eyes but let Casey continue.

"Marshmallow is my pet name for sexy ass over here. And what do you call me?"

She grinned impishly at Jess.

"Pain in the ass," her girlfriend retorted.

"Oh c'mon, you want to tell her," Casey cooed as she wrapped Jess up in an embrace.

"No I really don't."

"Well, you can tell her that or I can tell her what you and I did at Canopy Corp. Headquarters."

"Casey don't you dare!"

"Well..."

She looked at Jess expectantly.

Jess sighed.

"Fine. I call her Kit Kat, because she loves them and I used to get them for her all the time."

Casey beamed at Jess's confession. "And…"

Jess tried to look upset but I could tell she wasn't.

"And I love you, you little dork."

Casey kissed her deeply on the lips. "I love you too marshmallow!"

I couldn't help but smile too. It was obvious how much they cared about each other.

"You two are the most adorable couple ever."

"Thank you!" Casey exclaimed, still clinging to Jess's neck.

Jess smiled. She was obviously super-tough but had a soft side underneath.

"Um, so why do you have so much cum on you?" she asked me awkwardly.

Casey hit Jess playfully. "Now who's being too personal."

"Hey, it's a legitimate question."

I looked down at Kez's sauce all over my body mixed with my own sultry juices. My tentacle lover had remained hidden so far. I had told him to not show himself when people were around. I was afraid what would happen if people found out about him and decided to hunt or capture him.

So this was going to take some explaining.

"Um, so this may be a little hard to believe…"

"We just got fucked by zombies," Jess told me. "Trust me, we're up for believing anything."

"Oh yeah, that was… really hot."

"You were watching us?" Casey asked.

"Well, maybe."

"Oo, Jess, we were so hot, we made other people want to fuck."

"Great Case, I'll put that on my resume."

"You should!"

"First I want to hear who came all over our new friend

here."

Oh right. I was stalling.

"Okay, so…"

Wow. I was having a really hard time explaining this. Fuck it, showing is always easier than telling.

"Kez!" I yelled over the side. "You can come out now."

Kez's tentacles emerged from the water and loomed over the deck.

"Ahhhh!" Casey screamed as she hid behind Jess.

Jess used her body to protect Casey as she stared up at Kez.

I jumped between them and him. "Don't freak out. He won't hurt you."

"Um, is that your pet?" Casey asked as she clung to Jess's back.

"No. He's my boyfriend."

Both women's mouths dropped.

Jess took in the large tentacles. "Um, your what?"

"My boyfriend. Well, tenta-friend. I mean… he's my lover."

Kez ran his arms tenderly across my legs, waist, breasts, and cheek. I kissed the tip of his small tendril that brushed my lips.

"Oh my God," Jess and Casey said simultaneously.

"That is so freakin' hot! Real life hentai!" Casey said as her eyes went wide like an anime character.

Her hands moved unconsciously to Jess's tits and began playing with them. Jess still had her eyes glued on me and Kez, gripping Casey's forearm with one hand and rubbing her thigh with the other.

"You… can communicate with it?" Jess asked, seemingly not believing her eyes.

"With him, yes. His name is Kez."

"How do you, um, talk to him?" Casey piped in, now

19

pinching Jess's nipples lightly, eliciting cute, soft moans from her girlfriend.

"Oh, well, I…" Oh boy, this was going to be even more embarrassing. "Whenever he's inside me, I can understand him."

"You mean he sticks his tentacles in your…" Casey trailed off as she squeezed Jess's firm tits very hard.

"Ow, Casey!"

"Oops, I'm sorry! I'm just getting really turned on."

I could see Jess was as well as the moisture forming on her pussy lips was clear from here.

"So, yeah, he shoves his tentacles in my pussy. And… my ass."

Both women's eyes widened. Jess's hand moved toward her crotch. Casey once again squeezed her lover's golden globes but this time just the right amount as Jess cooed in delight from how her nipples were being tweaked.

"Ohhh Casey!"

Casey grabbed Jess's hand and yanked her closer to me and Kez.

"Oh my God! Jess and I just got to do anal for the first time recently too."

"Um, Case, we really don't need to share all our sexual escapades with her."

"Of course we do! That's how you make new friends!"

"What?! You are such a weirdo."

Casey kissed Jess on the cheek and embraced her tightly. "That's why you love me!"

Jess tried to frown but couldn't resist her adorable lover.

"Did you, um, do it… with those zombies?" I asked, intrigued and glad they didn't think I was strange for enjoying tentacles up my perky butt.

"Oh no. I, um… well, you see…"

She hesitated, looking at Jess.

Her athletic girlfriend sighed. "Oh just tell her."

"Okay! I fucked Jess's tight little hole with my huge cock."

Now it was my turn to gape at them with my mouth open.

"Um, you're what?"

"Oh it's a fun story. Well, it was actually really scary, but it all turned out okay. Jess you tell her."

Jess sighed again as Casey held her lovingly around the waist and rested her head on her shoulder.

Kez echoed her movements, squeezing my waist with one of his larger tendrils and brushing my cheek with a small one.

"Okay, so here's the deal," Jess began. "When we fucked some zombies and they jizzed inside us, it somehow gave Casey a big dick and made my pussy ultra-horny and in need of constantly being fucked. But then we finally found a cure just before we got turned into sex zombies."

"Buuuut," Casey picked up the tale. "Jess missed my super-zombie-cock in her super-cute, tight holes so we decided to get some zombie sauce in us again."

I stared blankly at them, trying to process everything. Man, and I thought fucking a tentacle creature was out there.

"So... does that mean you guys are going to become sex zombies?"

"Oh no," Casey answered in her chipper way. "We still have some of the antidote left. Right Jess?"

"Uh huh," Jess confirmed. "So where is it?"

"What do you mean?"

"The antidote. You have it."

"No I don't. You do."

"Oh my God! Case, you lost it?"

"No! You have it!"

"Where do you think I'm keeping it? Up my ass?"

Jess indicated her fully nude body. It would be pretty hard

to hide anything. Casey, nevertheless, peeked back at her irate girlfriend's super-toned ass.

"Casey! It's not in my ass."

"We must have lost it when we were fucking those zombies."

Jess groaned and covered her face with her hands. "We have to go back for it."

"Um," I interjected. "You might not want to do that."

I flicked my head back toward the dock. It was swarming with zombies.

"Shit!" Jess cursed.

"Jessss! I don't want to have a cock forever."

"I know sweetie. We'll figure something out."

As she pulled Casey into her and brushed her hair, I felt Kez's large tenta-cock pierce my lips and enter me.

"Uhhhhh!" I moaned, drawing the attention of both women as Kez tugged my thong down my thighs.

They looked at me and Kez like we were one of the hottest things they had ever seen.

"Oh wow," Casey gushed.

"Uh huh," Jess concurred.

I was rather embarrassed that I was being plundered right in front of them, but I could sense that Kez felt left out of the conversation and wanted to know what was going on. Which was understandable.

"He... he wants me to tell him about you two and what we've been, uhhhhh, talking about."

He had pushed even farther into me as I spoke, so he was fully against my cervix now, meaning we could communicate really well. It also meant I was starting to leak my fluids and getting horny as hell.

"Oh my God, it's so big," Jess observed in wonder.

"That must feel amazing in her pussy," Casey added.

I felt Kez massage all of my insides and pulse inside me. He wanted me to tell them how much I enjoyed him filling me.

"Uhhhh, yes it does!" I admitted.

Jess and Casey clutched each other, their hands drifting toward each other's dampening pussies.

I relayed all the relevant info to Kez. He seemed to take the existence of zombies in stride. They probably weren't really that much different than regular humans to him.

He then asked me something else.

"Kez! No, not in front of them."

"Not what in front of us?" Casey asked curiously with her bright blue eyes.

"I think he wants to fuck her," Jess told her.

That Jess was very perceptive.

"Oo, can you guys please fuck in front of us?" Casey asked endearingly.

"Ohhh," I groaned as Kez wormed around inside my very full cavern. "I don't think we should… uhhhh."

"Oh c'mon," Casey pleaded. "You got to watch us get our pussies pounded by those zombies. It's only fair we get to see your boyfriend fuck you with his huge tenta-cock!"

Hey, she came up with the same name for it I did. These girls were really on the same wavelength of me. And they were pretty damn adorable. Both individually and as a couple.

I could feel Kez tell me he thought I should totally listen to them. Of course, he loved every opportunity to pleasure me. Though I also got the sense he felt we could trust them and that it would make them want to fuck badly too.

Well, okay, why not?

"Uhhhh, o… okay. Kez go ahead and fuck me."

He pulsed inside me again.

"Yes! Please fuck me hard and make me your slut!"

Jess and Casey looked like they might cum right on the

spot.

"Jess?"

"Yeah?"

"I am so fucking wet right now."

"Me too."

Kez took that as his cue to start plunging in and out of my gorged hole.

I moaned loudly as he tied my hands above my head and thrust deliciously between my legs.

My tits bounced sensually as he filled me with his manhood.

Jess and Casey knelt on the deck and began rubbing each other's pussy lips. Their eyes riveted on the kinky sex show in front of them.

I sensed Kez ask me if he could make me really submissive in front of our new friends. I told him in my mind it was okay. Part of me was mortified at the idea. But another part wanted him to show Jess and Casey just how much of a tentacle slut I could be. And that part was apparently winning out.

He lifted me off the deck, pulled me off his cock, and let gravity spear me back down on it.

"Oh fuuuuck!" I screamed at being impaled on his tentacle that was so good at dominating me.

He kept lifting me up and letting me fall back down on his huge shaft. And every time I shrieked in overwhelming pleasure and felt my nectar run down my legs.

We were motivating Jess and Casey to increase their efforts. They now had multiple fingers deep inside each other's cute cunts and had their free hands roaming all over their lover's body.

They alternated between making out and stealing peeks at me and Kez, their lust increasing every time they saw my pussy get engorged.

My tits bounced spectacularly and I thought how kinky it was they were getting to see me made into Kez's sex toy. I didn't realize I enjoyed exhibitionism so much, but I was getting really turned on being made to perform in front of two extremely beautiful and sexy women.

I felt the cool, night breeze blow in from the water, but the intense fucking kept me warm.

Kez's tendrils wrapped around my ample breasts and squeezed them just the way I liked and tickled my extremely erect nipples.

"Ohhhhh Kez! It feels so fucking good. Please don't stop!"

I knew he had no intention of stopping. Even without my slutty moans, he could sense how much I wanted him to keep going. And go even harder.

He placed me back on the deck, this time on my knees, making sure my thighs were spread wide and he was as far into me as possible.

As I was groaning in delight, I heard something I definitely didn't expect.

"Fuck Casey, I need your huge cock so bad!"

Um, what?

I looked over and saw Casey now had a ridiculously large penis between her legs. When the hell did that happen? She didn't have that a minute ago. Of course, I always kind of lost track of time when Kez was pillaging my holes.

Jess was on her back with her knees up and legs spread and Casey was sliding her massive member into what I could only imagine was her girlfriend's very tight pussy.

"Ohhhhhhahhhhhh!" Jess screeched as she was penetrated.

"Jess, are you okay?" Casey asked worriedly.

"Y... yeah. God you're so big."

"Should I stop?"

"No. I need it. I need you. So fucking bad. Give me your

huge cock Case!"

"Okay, you got it marshmallow!"

Casey entered her lover's channel more fully, causing both of them to groan and moan.

Okay, that was really hot.

Kez could sense me getting more turned on and wrapped his arms around my hips and thighs and tied my arms behind my back, so he had complete control of my body.

He gyrated my hips, forcing me to fuck his wonderfully tasty cock. He kept thrusting my hips up and down, turning me into his personal fuck toy and making me squeal in ecstasy.

Casey and Jess were really going at it. Jess had her legs wrapped around Casey's cute butt as her fuck friend plowed her overfull pussy. They were both making some of the hottest sex faces I had ever seen. As I thought that, Kez informed me I made even sluttier faces. Gee, thanks Kez.

As my unique lover continued to rule my womanhood, I saw more of his tentacles grab Jess and Casey and flip them over, so Casey was on her back and Jess straddling her. They were in a very similar position to how Kez was fucking me.

Jess glanced up for a minute, surprised at the new position. Then shrugged her shoulders and began riding Casey for all she was worth. The younger woman reached up and grabbed both of her girlfriend's perky breasts as Jess's soaked pussy rammed down again and again on a behemoth of a cock.

Kez jackhammered me even harder, apparently also getting turned on by the two lovers in front of us. And I mean right in front of us. Kez had positioned them so Casey's head was near my knees. Which meant she had a great view of my pussy as it issued its sex juices. And I was eye-level with Jess who looked at me with a face that told me she was having the greatest sex of her life. I could definitely relate.

Kez matched my motions to Jess's, so we moved in

symmetry like sexual waves on an orgasmic ocean. It was pure bliss.

"Oh God Jess!" Casey yelled. "Your pussy, it's... so fucking tight... I can't believe it!"

"Uhhhhh, I know! You're filling every inch of me. Your cock owns my pussy! Please don't ever take it out!"

Oh wow. These two really knew how to do slutty talk right. I was getting just as good of a sex show as Kez and I were putting on for them.

Kez twisted and wormed his tenta-cock around inside me as he thrust me up and down on it, sending new sinful sensations through my whole body. He wanted me to talk smutty to him. With what he was doing to me, I really didn't have much of a choice.

"Oh fuck Kez! Yes! Dominate my pussy! Make me fuck your huge cock like the little sex toy I am!"

I saw both women look up at me, taking in my lustful body being plundered and my juices spilling out just above Casey's hair.

"Case, I need you to take me from behind!"

Casey immediately wrapped up Jess and fumbled around with her as their bodies got tangled. Then she put Jess on all fours and inserted her new penis back into Jess's waiting pussy, which I could see was beyond saturated with her sexy sauces.

Casey grabbed both of Jess's wrists and pulled them behind her, using them to yank Jess back hard onto her throbbing cock.

Kez pushed me forward and replicated the same position, seizing my arms and pulling me backwards onto his slimy shaft.

Jess and I were fucked doggy style by our lovers' huge members. And fucked hard. Jess's face was right in front of mine and I got an up close view of how she was being destroyed in sexual pleasure. I was feeling the same way and my epic sultry moans mixed with Jess's shrieks and Casey's groans to fill the clear night with an erotic concerto.

"Oh God Jess! I'm going to explode inside you!" Casey screamed.

"Just a little longer!" Jess pleaded. "I'm almost there too!"

Kez knew they were both about to cum so he increased to a speed I couldn't even process. What I did know is that every part of my pussy felt like it was going to erupt.

All three of us came at the same time. Our screams pierced the air as fluids flowed out of us like three huge sexual fountains.

From Casey's face and the way her body was twitching, I could tell she was spurting her seed into Jess. And a lot of it from what I could tell.

Jess's juices were spurting out around Casey's massive cock, soaking her thighs and the deck.

My nectar flew in a multitude of directions past Kez's massive manhood. My whole body shook from the climaxes detonating inside me.

Kez lifted me off the deck again, this time right over Jess and Casey. He pulled his cock out of me and seized my clit with two small tendrils, squeezing and flicking at it so my orgasms just kept coming.

I came all over Jess's back, creating strange patterns with my squirting sauce.

Casey yanked her cock out of Jess and spurted the rest of her seed across her lover's back, mixing it with my cum. Oh boy, we were really soaking Jess. I hoped she didn't mind.

Casey collapsed on top of Jess, getting the cum-mixture all over her tits and stomach. Meanwhile, I was still screaming and squirting, this time coating Casey's ass.

Kez laid me on top of Casey so the three of us were stacked on top of one another with Jess on the bottom. I came a little more and could feel it run down Casey's cute and supple bottom.

I could feel their bodies continue to twitch underneath me, and all three of us continued to issue a little more cum as our mini-post-orgasms wracked our bodies.

I felt Kez's tentacles move tenderly across my body and could see he was gently massaging the girls too. They didn't seem to mind.

We stayed that way for a while, content to lay in an ultimate post-sex sandwich.

"Um, Jess, I kind of came all over you," Casey admitted.

"I, um, sort of did too," I confessed.

"So, basically, you have a lot of cum on you," Casey concluded.

Jess panted, trying to catch her breath. "Don't worry about it. It's a lot better than being covered in zombie jizz."

"You've got that right!" Casey agreed.

We remained there. I rode the waves of Casey's body as she breathed in and out and Casey rode Jess's. I could sense from Kez that our curves all together looked like the most sensual of oceans.

I smiled. I forgot how poetic he could be.

Casey sighed contentedly underneath me. "I like being the meat in this super-sexy sandwich. You know because I'm in the middle and I have this huge salami between my legs."

Jess groaned. "Ugh, Casey. Your jokes are getting worse."

"Oh you still think I'm adorable."

"Maybe."

Casey kissed the back of Jess's neck, knowing her girlfriend was just giving her a hard time.

I knew we should probably get up, but man it felt really

comfortable being on top of them and Kez covering me with his caressing tendrils.

"So, your, um, penis," I began to ask, feeling really weird. "That's from the zombie jizz?"

"Yup," Casey replied, seemingly used to having a cock. "Though I think it might be even bigger this time."

"It is," Jess confirmed. She would definitely know better than anyone.

"I… I didn't hurt you, did I?" Casey asked worriedly.

"No sweetie it's fine. You were amazing. And I think the zombie cum is making me even hornier this time. I needed every inch of your sweet cock more than anything I've ever wanted in the world."

"Oh. Okay good!"

I smiled. These two were both super-sweet and super-hot. I could see why they made such a good couple.

"So Kione…" the effusive young woman I was laying on said. "Kez is, um, really good at slutting you up."

"Casey!" Jess admonished her.

"What? C'mon Jess, you know you were super-turned on by them."

"Well… maybe a little."

"Jessss." Now it was Casey's turn to scold Jess.

"Okay, okay. It was really freakin' hot and I want to see her tight pussy get filled by all his tentacles."

Oh my goodness. She wasn't kidding when she said the zombie jizz was making her ultra-horny.

"Shit. I'm sorry Kione. That was so wrong."

"Yeah, geez Jess, I never say stuff like that," Casey teased.

"Oh don't worry about it," I told Jess. "Honestly, I was having just as many lustful thoughts about you two and loved all the noises you made when Casey kept dominating you with her zombie cock."

"See? She's just as horny as we are, Jess."

I gasped as I felt Kez enter me. "Kez wants to know if you're okay that he has his tendrils over you."

"Oh sure, it feels really nice actually," Case replied.

"Yeah, it's... not as weird as I thought it would be," Jess added.

"Okay, good. He just wanted to make sure we were all warm enough."

The air was still a little chilly and Kez could emanate such a wonderful, soothing warmth through his tentacles.

Casey patted one of his tentacles. "Oh my God, he's so sweet. You have one awesome boy... um, tentacle-friend Kione."

"Thanks. He is pretty amazing."

I felt Kez pulse inside me, happy that I thought so fondly of him.

I asked the girls more about zombies, and they filled me in on their adventures. Jess told me she was part of an elite special forces unit called A.S.S.E.T. and that her former commander, whose name was Kresker, had secretly been working with a pharmaceutical company called Canopy Corp. They apparently developed some kind of virus that turned people into zombies, and Jess and Casey had been trying to survive their city being overrun by the undead.

I couple of weeks ago I would have said that was the most preposterous thing I had ever heard. But after meeting and becoming the lover of a sexy, tentacle creature, I wasn't going to dismiss anything, no matter how outlandish.

When they were in the middle of telling me a particular scandalous story of how they had to defeat Jess's evil former boss and a super-hot female scientist in a sex battle, Jess sprung up, knocking both me and Casey off her and onto the deck.

"I've got it!"

"Got what?" Casey asked. "I was really comfy laying on you."

"You can use me as a pillow as much as you want later, promise. But I know where there might be more of the antidote."

Casey's eyes lit up. "You do?"

"Yeah, I just remembered Kresker had a secret hideout. I followed him to it one time when he started acting weird. But I never went inside. He might have kept some of the antidote there."

"Great! Let's go get it!"

They looked at me hopefully.

"Yes, of course I'll help," I told them. "Can't have you guys becoming sex zombies."

Casey threw her arms around me. "You're the best Kione!"

She pulled Jess into the hug, and I felt two fabulous pairs of breasts press against me as well as wonderfully smooth and sensual legs and thighs.

And I also felt Kez expand deeper inside me.

"Uhh, Kez says he would like to help too."

"Sure," Jess said, eyeing the large, throbbing tentacle between my lips. "We could use all the help we can get."

Casey thrust her fist into the air. "Super-Sluts Assemble!"

"Okay, that is not what we are calling ourselves," Jess told her firmly.

"Wonder Whores?"

"Nope."

"Crazy Cumming Chicks?"

"Uh uh."

"Super-Sexy Bisexual Horny Women Who Sometimes Have Cocks?"

"Accurate. But way too wordy."

"What about Lust Hunters?" I suggested.

Casey's eyes glowed. "Oo, that's really good."

She looked at Jess.

"Okay, fine."

Casey tossed her hand in the air again. "Lust Hunters Assemble!"

She looked at us expectantly.

"Hey, c'mon, you guys have to do it too."

Jess sighed. Which I had learned was her giving in to her cute girlfriend's zany requests.

Casey counted to three and we all raised our fists.

"Lust Hunters Assemble!" we cried out as Kez joined us by lifting one of his tentacles in the air.

Well, it wasn't exactly the Justice League or the Avengers, but it was way sexier.

Guess we had an antidote to find.

CHAPTER THREE

Fortunately, Kresker's hideout was on an inlet of the bay, so we could take my yacht there and Kez could accompany us. I definitely didn't want to leave him behind.

As we puttered around the large bay, I could see Jess and Casey through the wheelhouse window. I saw Jess stagger against the railing and Casey drop to her knees.

"Kez, take the wheel!" I both thought and shouted to him. He had been inside me so he understood. I had dispensed with bothering to wear anything to give Kez easy access and to make my new naked friends feel more comfortable. I had also gotten very used to the feeling of him residing within my pussy and ass. Sometimes it was to make sweet, crazy-intense tentacle love to me. Other times, he just wanted to be with me. And being inside my tender folds was how he could be close to me and share intimate thoughts. So I spent good portions of the day walking around with some nice tentacles in my pussy, ass, or sometimes both. But it did let me bond with Kez in a way I never had with any previous partner. I felt a really strong connection to him and was so happy I found him in that cave.

He slipped out of my pussy and took the wheel as I dashed out to the girls. As I got near the bow, I saw Casey's penis get erect right before my eyes. Oh my. It was quite an impressive sight seeing her massive cock grow between her legs and get rock hard.

Jess dropped to the deck beside her, clutching the railing.

"What's wrong?" I asked, worried the zombie jizz was having some adverse effect on them.

"The zombie cum is… making me so fucking horny and wet I… can barely stand," Jess informed me between gasps.

"And I can't control this freakin' mutant cock!" Casey whined.

Damn. It hadn't been that long since they had fucked each other and they were already so much hornier and out of control. That zombie jizz was really powerful.

"Case, I… I need you to fuck me again."

"Oh God yes Jess! Get that tight little pussy over here."

Jess crawled across the deck. Fuck, watching this was really hot. Kez thought so too as I could sense his thoughts as he wormed his way into me again.

"No, I… I need it in my ass. The cum must be making me need it there super-bad this time."

"Oh God I want to marshmallow but I'm so fucking big."

I could see Casey's cock throbbing between her legs. Like it needed to be in either Jess's warm pussy or tight ass to find that sweet release it craved.

"Fuck Case I don't care! I have to be fucked right now. I can't take it anymore. I know you'll be gentle. You always are. That's just one reason I love you so much."

"Awww, Jess, you're going to make me cry. I love you a million-billion times! Now turn around so I can fuck that super-hot ass of yours!"

That was one of the sweetest, and strangest, conversations I had witnessed.

Kez brought a blanket out of the cabin and handed it to Jess and Casey.

"Aw thanks Kez," Casey beamed at him as Jess quickly spread the blanked out and got on her hands and knees, wiggling her perfect ass in front of Casey.

"Ohhh, Case, please... my ass."

"Okay! I'm sorry if this hurts a little. I love you!"

"I love you t... ahhhhhhhhhhhhhhhh!"

Jess's reply was cut off as Casey's huge head penetrated Jess's tiny hole.

"I'm sorry!"

"No, it's... oh God Case, you're cock, it's amazing! Give me more of it!"

I didn't think I was ever going to have to watch porn again after this. I could just replay this scene in my memory. Or just have Kez fuck me in all the delicious, submissive ways he was so good at.

Jess groaned and gasped as Casey inched farther and farther into her. Both women were making faces of people completely lost in sexual rapture.

And then I found myself on my hands and knees, another blanket underneath me, and Kez slipped one of his tendrils inside my ass.

"Oh fuck Kez!"

It was a little larger than the one he normally put in there. He must have sensed my thoughts, watching Jess and Casey's super-hot anal fucking. Seeing how large Casey's cock was in Jess's very fuckable ass, I was thinking what it might feel like if Kez used a bigger tentacle on me.

And now I knew. It felt amazing. It was an extremely tight fit. And a little uncomfortable at first. But Kez always knew the best way to worm around inside me to make it pleasurable. I'm sure it helped that he could read my reactions to what he was doing inside me and could adjust to make sure it was as pleasurable as possible. This telepathic-type link could be really handy at times.

He pulled my arms behind my back and tied my hands there. While also lassoing my hips and thighs and pulling me back onto his cock that was so delightfully filling my ridiculously tiny cavern.

Right in front of me, I could see Casey thrusting harder into Jess, who was somehow taking almost all of her lover's zombie cock.

"Ohhhh Jess! Your ass is making my cock go crazy!"

"Ahhhh Casey! Please make me the biggest anal slut in the universe!"

Okay, so it was impossible not to be turned on beyond belief watching and listening to these two. Kez began plowing my ass harder, and I groaned and moaned louder as my muscles clenched around his slick shaft.

Casey snatched Jess's arms and held them in place behind her back, making Jess put her face down on the blanket. I knew this meant Casey could get even farther into Jess's new favorite fuckhole. The young woman grabbed both of Jess's arms tightly, using them for leverage as she plundered her lover's ass.

Kez placed me in the same position, my ass sticking up provocatively, and I felt him burrow even deeper into my small cave. While a smaller tentacle teased my clit and made my legs shake.

Both Casey and Kez increased their thrusting, owning our asses like no one had before.

"Oh God I'm going to cum!" Casey screamed.

"Yes do it!" Jess replied at equally slutty decibels. "Fill my ass with your sweet cum!"

I could feel Kez ask a question and I sensed he was also on the verge of exploding.

"Yes Kez yes! I want you to cum inside my ass. Make me take all of your tentacle juices!"

That did it. He couldn't contain himself any longer, especially when I talked to him like such a good little whore.

I felt his tentacle open up and his sweet seed shoot into me. I squirmed around as my own orgasm exploded inside me. Fuck, he was squirting so much of his sauce into my ass. And that was just making me spurt my own juices even more.

I glanced up and could tell Casey was unloading a ridiculous amount of her jizz inside Jess's sultry ass.

"Ohhhhhhhhhhhhhhhhh!" Jess moaned as her girl juices splattered the blanket underneath her.

"Ahhhhhhhhhhhhhhhhhh!" Casey groaned as she emptied her mutant cock into her lover.

"Uhhhhhhhhhhhhhhhhhh!" I screamed as Kez made me cum even harder from the attention he was paying my ass and clit.

Casey and Kez let us both go at the same time, and Jess and I landed on our stomachs on the blankets.

Then our lovers took their cocks out of our asses and spurted the rest of their jizz over our asses and backs.

Jess's head was right next to mine and I could tell by the way she was twitching she was still having serious orgasms. I was as well, spasming sensually next to Jess.

Casey eventually collapsed on top of Jess, and Kez wrapped me up in his loving tendrils.

I knew it sucked these two had zombie jizz inside them that was making them super-sluts. But man it was inspiring me and Kez to have some of the most epic sex ever. I wondered after we got them the antidote if they'd still be down with this quasi-group sex idea. Because it was pretty freaking hot.

When I had finally recovered from Kez's sultry anal probing, I scooted inside the wheelhouse and steered us toward our destination.

Jess pointed out an old house on a bank above the water. I pulled into a small dock below it and Kez tied us off.

"Okay," Jess stated, naturally falling into take-charge mission mode. "I'll go in and see if I can find the antidote. You three wait here and watch out for zombies."

"What?!" Casey replied, alarmed. "No way! I'm going with you."

"Case, I want to make sure you're safe."

"Jess, I'm only safe when I'm with you."

Jess's tough visage faltered, touched by how much Casey wanted to be with her."

"I'm coming too," I chipped in before Jess could protest further.

Kez immediately wrapped me up so I couldn't move and entered me deeply.

"Ohh Kez! What's wrong?"

He didn't want me to go. Like Jess worrying about Casey, he was afraid something would happen to me. It was awfully sweet of him.

"Sweetie, slip into my ass too." When we had this heart-to-hearts, I always had him inside me as much as possible so we could have an extremely intimate conversation with no misunderstandings.

He punctured my little hole and I could feel his essence surrounding me. One of total love and devotion. It honestly was even nicer than all the mind-blowing sex we had.

"I love that you're so worried about me but remember I go on dangerous adventures all the time."

He pulsed inside me.

"I know, I know. Yes you can often be there with me now. But there will be places I have to go that you can't follow, because they're on land. I can take care of myself."

I could feel that he didn't understand why anyone would let their lover go off on their own. It was one of those human-tentacle creature cross-species differences. We had already run into a few of those since we started dating, but we always managed to work it out.

"Okay, so human beings do really enjoy and need to be with others, especially those they love. But we also sometimes need to be on our own and go do our own thing. And we need our loved ones to trust and believe in us."

He kind of understood that. But had a question.

"Well, yeah, we still worry about our loved ones. I know that kind of sucks. But it's part of being in a relationship."

He told me he didn't realize human relationships were this complicated.

I chuckled. "Oh trust me sweetie, they totally are. But they're also worth it. And being with you is totally worth it. I've kind of fallen hard for you."

He squeezed me more tightly, alarmed.

I laughed again. "No, no. Not falling down. It's a human saying. It means I really love you."

He relaxed but kept squeezing me. This time in an adoring and gratified way.

I took one of his tiny tendrils and kissed its tip. He slipped it inside me and we French kissed.

He eased his grip on me, and I glanced over to Jess and Casey.

Casey had tears in her eyes.

"Oh my God, tentacle-love is so beautiful!" she half-cried/half-gushed at seeing our loving interactions.

Jess took her in her arms and wiped away her tears. Jess was much better at concealing her emotions but I could tell even she was moved by how much Kez and I meant to each other.

She kissed Casey lovingly.

"Okay, you both can come. But you need to follow my lead and do what I say."

I nodded.

"You got it chief!" Casey replied. "You're in charge on scary, zombie missions. I'm in charge when you want me to tie you up and treat like you like a super-slut."

Jess rolled her eyes. "Casey, I'm going to throw you in the bay."

"Oo, that's not a bad idea," her mischievous friend said, unperturbed. "We're all still covered in cum, so we could use a good bath."

With that, Kez snatched us all by the waist or ankle, yanked us off the ship, and dunked us in the cold water.

Jess, Casey, and I all shrieked from the surprise soaking.

"Ahhhhhh!"

"Kez!!"

"Oh my God that's freaking cold!"

He held us upside down over the bay and used his tentacles to suck up the water. And then spray us off like a firehose.

We screamed and sputtered louder as we got washed like a car.

When he put us back on the deck, we stood holding ourselves and shivering.

He handed towels to Jess and Casey and began drying me off. The two girls dried each other. At first tenderly, then a little more roughly as they horseplayed.

"Sorry about that," I said when my teeth had stopped chattering. "He likes to do surprise dunkings like that. He can be pretty sneaky."

"Oh that's okay," Casey said amiably. "At least we're all cleaned off."

"And maybe the cold shower will help keep our raging hormones in check," Jess added.

Casey tousled her hair with the towel. "Oh good point marshmallow."

Jess tossed the towel aside and took Casey's hand, leading her toward the dock.

"Okay, let's go find an antidote."

I kissed Kez one last time and hopped off the boat after them.

CHAPTER FOUR

We climbed up the bank and the steep steps leading to the house. It looked like something right out of a horror movie. I was usually pretty fearless exploring ancient crypts, hidden caves, and predator-infested jungles in my treasure-hunting profession, but I wasn't so big on haunted houses. At least not real haunted houses that probably had zombies inside them.

Casey must have been feeling the same way. She clung to Jess's side.

"Um, do we really have to go in there?"

"Case, you realize we've been in a ton of scary, zombie-infested places the past few days, right?"

"Well yeah, but this one is extra spooky."

Jess squeezed her shoulder. "Just stay close to me."

"Absolutely!"

She hopped behind Jess and wrapped her arms around her, pressing her creamy tits tightly against Jess's back.

"That might be a little too close."

"Tough." Casey hugged Jess even tighter.

Jess sighed.

"Okay, let's go in."

She headed for the front door, Casey shuffling to keep up.

I smiled, realizing how cute they looked. And how

especially cute Casey's butt looked as she scurried to keep pace with Jess.

I looked up at the creaking house as the wind picked up and I felt raindrops begin to fall. Perfect. Well, time to explore the haunted house that I was sure didn't have any zombies in it.

I really wished Kez was here.

I hurried to catch up with my new zombie-hunting friends. Jess was just opening the door when I reached them. It groaned open in a perfectly creepy way. Oh c'mon. This was ridiculous. Now I was really feeling like we were walking into a slasher flick. And we had already proved many times today that none of us were virgins, so we were all in trouble.

Casey poked her head over Jess's shoulder and I peeked over Casey's. It was extremely dark inside the house. I could barely make out anything.

As we all peered inside the super-spooky house, a huge blast of thunder ripped through the air. We all yelled and rushed inside the house.

Casey replastered herself to Jess's back and I joined in, clutching Casey's shoulders and pressing my sizeable tits against her smooth back.

"Um, I… want to make sure I don't lose you guys in the dark," I stammered, making up a lame excuse.

"Smart," Casey replied, apparently totally fine I had my private parts glued to her back and supple bottom.

"Oo, your body's nice and warm," she continued.

"Um, thanks."

"Oh, I've been meaning to ask. You're so freakin' beautiful. Are you Middle Eastern?"

"I'm Egyptian."

"Oh cool! What's it like in-"

"Hey!" Jess interrupted. "You can get Kione's life story

later. We're kind of on a mission here."

"Oh don't be jealous marshmallow. You know you're the most gorgeous, amazing, sexiest woman in the world for me and the only one I want to be with."

She squeezed Jess tightly and kissed her on the cheek.

"I'm not jealous!" Then she took a deep breath, realizing she was sounding a little jealous. "I agree Kione's crazy beautiful. I just want to keep you guys safe. And we all need to be looking out for zombies."

Casey kissed her again. "You're my superhero! And aye aye Captain! Ten-four on the zombie lookout."

Jess glanced back at her. "You are so weird."

"Thanks!" Casey replied good-naturedly and delivered another sweet smooch.

The more I watched these two lovebirds, the more I missed Kez. Wow, I really had fallen super-hard for him. I wanted to spend every minute cuddling with his sweet tendrils. Huh, who would have thought my closest relationship would be with a tentacle creature.

I turned my attention back to the two sexy nude nymphs in front of me.

"So, um, thanks for all that super-nice things you guys said about me. You're both really sweet."

Casey turned back to me. "No problem!"

"And, um… thanks for letting me watch you two have sex. You guys fucking is like the hottest thing I've ever seen in my life."

"Yes! Hear that Jess, we're so sexy we could be porn stars."

"Oh great Case, that's what I've always wanted to become."

"What about a zombie porn star? You do really enjoy an undead dick inside you."

"Casey!" Jess scolded her. Then she looked like she was

thinking about it for a minute. "Fine, I'll do porn with you only if it's lesbian porn and you and me get to do a lot of kinky bondage."

"Wait, what?"

"Yeah, after this is all over, let's make a porno together."

For once, Casey was at a loss for words.

"Um, Jess, I was just kid…"

She trailed off as she saw a mischievous grin on her lover's face.

"Gotcha," Jess teased gleefully.

"Hey, no fair!" Casey complained.

"Oh please, you tease me all the time. I'm entitled to get you every so often."

Casey pouted. "Okay, that's… pretty fair actually. Oo, what if we just pretended we were making porn? You know, come up with ridiculous scenes and act like porn stars?"

"Um, sure. Though I think we've already been surpassing most porn by fucking zombies, becoming sex addicts, and watching a tentacle creature plunder every inch of our new friend."

I blushed. That was a very accurate statement.

"Oh yeah," Casey chirped. "Kione, you and Kez are so fucking hot! Jess and I were talking about how much we love making love when we watch you guys."

I blushed even more.

"Oh, um, thanks. I'm glad you enjoyed it. Kez is an amazing lover."

"No doubt!"

"Guys!" Jess slightly admonished. "If we keep talking about kinky fucking, I won't be able to control my ultra-horniness. I can already feeling it building again."

"Oh right. Yeah, my cock is getting hard too."

And I realized my thighs were a little wet. I wasn't even

jacked up on the zombie juice, but all this sex talk was turning me on. It also didn't hurt that I was pressed against two extremely beautiful, sexy ladies. Both of whom I was becoming quite fond of. In a friends-who-get-naked-all-the-time-but-are-just-friends way. Kez was absolutely the one I wanted to be with intimately.

Jess fumbled along the nearest wall and found a light switch. I heard her flick it, and the room was dimly illuminated by lights that seemed to understand the rules of horror movies: cast as little light as possible and flicker like crazy. Stupid lights.

We crept forward slowly. All still huddled together. I could see Jess's taut muscles as she constantly scanned the room and hallway in front of us. She would make an excellent adventurer and treasure hunter.

"Why did Kresker have to pick such a creepy hideout?" Casey asked.

"Well, it fits his personality," Jess replied.

Casey giggled. "That's true. Hey, what do you think happened to him?"

"Hopefully, a zombie bit him in the ass."

I could tell from the way she said it this Kresker guy was pretty much her least favorite person in the world.

"That would be funn... ah, what's that?!" Casey exclaimed mid-sentence.

"It's okay Kit Kat, it's just the floorboards creaking. Nothing to wo-"

Before she could finish, the floor collapsed underneath us.

We screamed as we plummeted into the basement, landing in a heap in small pool of water. I groaned and moved my limbs, making sure nothing was broken. As I did, I realized my hand was on Jess's unbelievably toned and sexy ass. And Casey's face was right inbetween my breasts.

She looked up at me. "Um, hi. Your boobs really cushioned my fall well."

I turned a slight shade of crimson. "Well, your girlfriend's perfect ass helped shield me from injury."

"Oh yeah, her ass is good for so many things. Hey, Jess, you okay down there?"

We heard Jess groan in response and mutter something about two people lying on top of her.

Oops. We rolled off Jess and helped her up. She had some scrapes and a bruise on her thigh, but I had a feeling she was very used to getting banged up in her job saving the world.

Casey rushed over to her, tenderly touching her bruise and a cut on her cheek.

"Oh Jess!"

Jess took her girlfriend's hands in hers. "Case, it's nothing really. Are you okay?"

"Oh yeah, I'm fine."

Jess turned to me. "Kione?"

"What? Oh yes. I'm all good. Sorry I, um, fell on you."

"Don't worry about it. I can imagine a lot worse things than two beautiful naked women falling on top of me."

I could too.

"Hey you little flirt!" Casey mock scolded her.

"What?" Jess responded innocently. "You do it too."

"Okay, fine," Casey agreed. "Just do most of your flirting with me."

"There's no one else I want to do it with."

She took Casey's face in her hands and kissed her passionately.

I tried to look away and whistle. But they just kept going at it. So I decided I might as well look around the room while the hot smooching was going on.

There was a couple of inches of stagnant water. The

basement must have been close enough to the bay that it had been partially flooded.

I found an overhead light and pulled the cord, bathing the basement in a soft, yellow glow.

I saw what looked like a makeshift lab with vials and chemicals and a couple of computer terminals.

"Hey guys, I think I found..."

I trailed off as I spun around and saw Jess and Casey.

They weren't kissing any more.

They were fucking.

Hard.

Jess was riding Casey's monster cock like the biggest cowgirl slut in the West. Her tits bounced as Casey put her hands on Jess's hips and guided her repeatedly onto her pulsating shaft.

Oookay.

"Um, guys..."

"Uhhhhhh... yeah, Kione?" Jess asked as she gyrated her hips harder onto Casey.

"I think the antidote might be over here."

"Great. I... ohhhhhh... just need to fuck the shit out of this little nympho first."

"And I... oh God... need to fill this slut's cunt with every ounce of my cum," Casey added.

"Hey... oh fuck... language Casey."

"Sorry... sweet Jesus... marshmallow. I... oooooooo... think the zombie cum is taking over."

"Holy fucking zombie cock! Me too!"

So okay, I was so fucking wet watching and listening to this. The way they were moaning and uttering super-slutty stuff as they were trying to talk was turning me on something fierce.

I was reaching for my tits and pussy when I heard

something.

Moaning. But not the sultry moans of my two nymphomaniac friends. Rather the really creepy zombie kind.

Shit.

I backed up toward Jess and Casey, looking around for something I could use as a weapon.

"Jess! Casey!" I tried to whisper-yell. "I think there are zombies coming."

"Great. They can join in," Jess whimpered.

I glanced back and saw they were now standing, Casey plowing Jess against a wall. Her delicious cock slamming fully into Jess's horny pussy again and again.

Damn, how did they switch positions so fast? These two really knew how to fuck.

I scooted over to them, hoping I could snap them out of it. It was a little awkward standing right next to them while they were fucking. But it did give me one hell of a view. I could clearly see Casey's cock sliding in and out of her lover's pussy, Jess's lips spread wide for it, her juices coating Casey's shaft.

Oh boy, I really needed to do something or I was going to become a sex zombie too.

"Listen I know you're both out of control needing to fuck each other, but I really need you guys to come to your senses."

Casey looked at me. "She's right Jess."

I exhaled. Thank goodness.

"There's a much better position I can fuck you in."

Casey grabbed Jess around the waist and spun her over to a shaky wooden table, bending her over it and ramming her dick back into its tight home.

Okay, so that didn't work as well as I hoped.

"Oh fuck, you're right Case this is so much better!" Jess screamed. "You're so fucking deep inside me!"

"God Jess I love your pussy! I love it more than anything.

Tell me how much you want me to fill it."

"Uhhhhhhhh! Yes! Fuck yes! Casey, squirt your sweet, sticky cum into me. Make me take every last inch of you like a good little whore!"

Okay, seriously, this was a thousand times better than porn.

And then the zombies started pouring in. Or more like falling in.

They dropped through the hole in the ceiling, got up, and staggered toward us.

I flung my hand out, trying to get the girls' attention, and wound up patting Jess repeatedly on the ass.

"Um, guys, zombies. Lots of zombies. Less fucking and more ass kicking please!"

Jess looked up from her pussy getting pounded and saw five really ugly creatures lurching toward us.

"Casey, new position!" she shouted.

She stood up, spun around to face Casey, and hopped up, wrapping her arms around her neck and her legs around her waist. Somehow she leapt perfectly so she landed right back on Casey's gigantic cock and slid all the way down it.

"Oh fuck!!!" Jess squealed at being impaled by her girlfriend.

Casey grabbed Jess's hips and lifted her up and down on her shaft, eliciting more squeals from her sex-crazed friend.

I wasn't sure how that was going to help us defeat the zombies, but then saw Jess grab a broom leaning against the wall. She unscrewed the end of it, so she now had a makeshift staff. She began bashing the zombies in their ugly faces. While she continued to fuck Casey.

Damn. This girl was talented.

She instructed Casey to spin her around as she kept spearing her onto her dick. She twirled the broomstick around, striking zombies left and right.

I realized I shouldn't let her have all the fun. At least in terms of the zombie bashing.

I spotted a shovel against another wall and snatched it up. I whacked the nearest zombie in her putrid face and then took some powerful swings to the new group of zombies that had just dropped through the hole.

"Uhhhh, Casey! I have to cum so bad. Fuck me harder!"

Casey complied, ramming her cock as hard as she could up into Jess's core. As she got closer to climaxing, it seemed it just made Jess even more of a badass. She swung the broom with even more power, nearly taking the zombies' heads off. They were knocked back into each other and fell like dominoes.

I was holding my own, striking zombies in their undead dicks and sweeping their legs out from underneath them.

I felt something clammy clasp my ankle. I looked down and saw a zombie on the floor had grabbed me. And was about to bite into my soft flesh.

"Ahhh!" I yelled as I repeatedly bashed the shovel onto his head until he stopped moving.

"Good... oh my God... job Kione!" Jess called out amid her pleasure moans. "Keep going for the head. That's how you keep them down for good."

To demonstrate, Jess hauled off with the broomstick and hit a zombie so hard his head spun around and cracked. He fell to the floor, lifeless. Well, he was already lifeless. Undeadless? Anyway, he wasn't going to bother us anymore.

I followed her lead and whacked the zombies in the head as hard as I could. The metal shovel proved a pretty effective anti-zombie weapon.

There was a few tense moments, but we managed to take out all of them.

I leaned on the handle of the shovel, trying to catch my breath. I didn't realize zombie hunting was such good exercise.

Jess and Casey were even more out of breath. But that's because they were still fucking each other's brains out.

Casey leaned back against a wall and continued to raise Jess up and down. The expert zombie hunter squeezed Casey tightly with her thighs and let her younger lover fuck her as hard as she wanted.

No matter how hard Casey rammed her, Jess didn't seem to be satiated.

"Oh God Casey! I need my ass filled too!"

"Uhhhhh, I'd love to finger your hot ass, but my hands are a little preoccupied."

She snatched Jess's hips even tighter and slammed her monster cock into her ferociously.

"Holy fuck!" Jess screamed in reply. "Okay, Kione, it's up to you."

I gaped at her. "Um, what's up to me?"

"Fucking my tight ass!"

"What?!"

"I won't be able to cum unless my ass gets fucked hard too. I know it's... ohhhhhhh... ridiculous. But I... fuck... can't think of anything else until I cum."

Okay, I definitely wasn't prepared for that kind of request.

"Case, are you... uhhhhhh... okay if..."

"Ahhhh! Yes! I know you can't control your ass lust. Kione you have permission to... ohhhhhh... finger my girlfriend's ass."

"If you're... good God... comfortable with that," Jess added as she clung to Casey for dear life.

I was definitely comfortable fucking someone as incredibly sexy as Jess. I just didn't want to be unfaithful to Kez.

But I had learned that because of the zombie jizz inside them, the girls needed to cum hard to get it briefly out of their system. Otherwise they would be able to do nothing except fuck nonstop and we'd eventually be overwhelmed by zombies.

Okay. To save our cute, naked bodies, I needed to finger this amazingly perfect ass. I just hoped Kez would understand.

I approached them tentatively as Jess's sexy butt continued bobbing up and down on Casey's shaft.

They were moaning non-stop now. They seemed to have almost completely lost themselves to their sex zombie fuckfest.

I knew Jess had had multiple things in her ass tonight, including Casey's throbbing salami, but I still didn't want to penetrate her tight hole without some lubrication.

Well, Jess was providing plenty of natural lube. I could see her juices leaking out of her ridiculously engorged pussy.

I rubbed my finger in them and then positioned it over her cute little hole.

"Oh God Kione! Shove it in my ass!"

Shit. Guess I was doing this.

I pressed into her and pierced her tightness. Her ass immediately clenched around my finger, like it was never letting go.

"Oh fuck yes! Stick it all the way in! I need it as deep as possible!"

Oh God this was hot. I pushed forward until my entire middle finger was inside her. Her ass was so fucking tight. And it had a death grip on my finger.

"Ohhhhhhhhhhh yes! That feels so fucking good! Now fuck it! I need my pussy and ass destroyed!"

Whoa. And I thought I got out of control sexually when Kez was dominating me.

I finger fucked her sexy hole, gradually building up speed. Casey was treating her pussy like her personal sex toy, spearing Jess like her sex zombie conquest.

The whole thing was so freaking hot the fingers of my other

hand were deep inside my pussy before I even knew it.

"Ohhhh fuck," I moaned as I anally probed Jess ridiculously hard.

The harder I fucked her, the more she screamed and begged for it.

And Casey was just as into it. "Oh God Jess, you're the biggest fucking whore in the universe!"

"I know!" Jess immediately agreed. "I'm a total slut! Pump my pussy with your zombie jizz and make me cum until I can't take it anymore!"

That really made Casey determined to unleash her seed into Jess. I couldn't believe how fast and hard she was jackhammering Jess. I tried to match it with my finger plundering. Of both Jess's ass and my now soaked pussy.

I saw Casey's eyes roll back in her head. Felt Jess's ass clench my finger even harder than it had before. And then felt both women's bodies shake as they came.

My own climax was just behind them. I pulled my fingers out and rapidly rubbed my clit, making sure I could issue as much cum as possible.

I kept my finger inside Jess because, quite frankly, I couldn't get it out. Her ass muscles had contracted around it so tightly I honestly couldn't pull it out. Talk about buns of steel.

Well, I was happy to leave it in that cozy spot as I let loose a flood of my juices.

All three of us moaned and screamed together. Casey was filling Jess with a torrent of zombie jizz. Jess was shooting out her sexy girl sauce all over the place.

When Casey finally pulled out of Jess, she lost her grip on her, and all three of us tumbled to the ground.

Our cum went everwhere. Casey's jizz squirted all over my tits. Jess's juices splattered my ass. Mine somehow got on both of them.

By the end of the marathon orgasm session, all three of us had everyone's cum all over our bodies.

This was my new favorite way to make new friends.

"Oh Case, the way you fucked me," Jess panted as we lay with our limbs entangled.

"I know, it was..." Casey sighed.

Jess touched my shoulder. "Kione, thanks for, well..."

"No problem," I replied. "I'm always happy to finger hot asses jacked up on zombie jizz."

Casey giggled. Jess blushed a little but couldn't help smiling too.

"So... are you guys relatively back to normal now?"

"Yes, but it won't last long," Jess told me.

"Yeah, it's going to keep getting worse until we can't do anything except fuck each other constantly if we don't find the antidote," Casey added.

I took a moment to imagine that. Well, maybe a few moments.

I hopped up. "Okay, well let's go take a look at all this sciency stuff over here before more zombies come."

I offered a hand to both girls and hauled them to their feet. They both stumbled a little and grabbed onto me to right themselves. I wasn't surprised they had a hard time standing after the ridiculously intense sex session they had.

We hurried over to the lab section and scanned the vials.

Jess snatched a small one. "This it it!"

Casey peered over her shoulder and read the label. "Yes! Good job Jess!"

I let out a breath. "Awesome. Can we leave the super-spooky house now?"

Jess searched the table some more. "Absolutely. We just need to find a jet injector to administer the antidote."

As we poured over the lab, we heard loud creaking above

us.

"Uh oh," Casey said as we all looked up. "More creepers."

I was about to go retrieve my handy shovel when the rest of the ceiling collapsed, bringing down the wooden floorboards and putrid flesh eaters.

We took cover under the lab table, huddling together as the rubble and undead fell all around us.

Oh this was so bad. There were so many more zombies than before. And we were completely cut off from our makeshift weapons.

Jess handed the vial to Casey. "Case, put this somewhere safe. We can't lose this."

She leaned forward on her hands and knees, getting ready to spring into action.

Casey looked over her naked body. Realized she had nowhere to hide the vial. Then looked at Jess's cute butt right in front of her.

And then shoved the vial right up Jess's ass.

"Holy shit!" Jess yelped in surprise. "Casey, what the hell?"

"You said put it somewhere safe."

"I didn't say stick it in my ass!"

"Sorry I panicked! But it is super-tight in there, so it won't fall out."

She gave Jess a cute, chagrined look.

"That's the problem. It's stuck in me so tightly I'm getting super-turned on again. How am I supposed to fight these zombies when all I can think about is being fucked up the ass?"

"Oops." Casey gave Jess one of her adorable apology smiles.

Jess sighed.

"Do you want me to shove it in a little farther?" Casey

asked helpfully.

Jess rolled her eyes. Then bit her lip. "Okay, fuck, yes."

Casey inserted her finger into Jess's tight hole and pushed.

"Uhhhh," Jess groaned.

"Fuck, Jess," Casey cooed. "Your ass is the hottest thing in the universe."

I couldn't disagree with that. I could feel my own body heat rising again from watching Casey using Jess's ass as a transportation receptacle.

The zombies who had fallen from the floor above had staggered to their feet.

We leapt up and dodged the closest ones. But really had nowhere to go.

We got backed into a corner. Over a dozen drooling denizens of the undead lurching toward us.

"Um, Jess?" Casey clutched her arm.

"I'm thinking!" Jess replied.

I was also scanning the room, trying to come up with a way out of this.

"Should we put on a slutty sex show for them like last time?" Casey asked.

I gaped at them. "I'm sorry, what?"

"We might not have much of a choice," Jess replied.

I wasn't sure how fucking each other would save us from the zombies. But we were about five seconds away from getting our asses bitten, so I was up for pretty much anything that would save us from joining the legion of the walking dead.

Just then I felt a voice in my head. Kez's voice. It was telling me to duck.

I yanked Jess and Casey to the floor. "Get down!"

The wall behind us crumbled and tentacles shot through.

It was Kez!

He snatched the zombies with his many tendrils and flung

them out of the opening he had made.

I peered out the hole and saw them plunge into the bay. I saw Kez's body partially up on land. The basement was low enough that he was able to crawl out of the water and reach his tendrils up to reach us.

But how did he know we were in trouble? And how did he communicate with me without touching me or being inside me? Maybe we were forming some kind of telepathic bond. The more he fucked me and was inside my pussy and ass could be strengthening our connection to each other. Wow. Talk about a close relationship. I guess we really were a good match.

The zombies scream-moaned in their creepy way as Kez continued to hurl them into the cold water.

But even more were coming in from above and with the small hole in the wall he could only snatch a couple at a time. Which meant some were going to get us.

We kicked the nearest zombies in the head as I tried to communicate with Kez we needed to get out of there now.

He scooped all of us up around our waists and pulled us out of the decrepit house. And then flung his body and us into the water, just barely avoiding the zombies trying to bite us.

We plunged into the bay. And even though I could immediately feel the chill through my naked body, I was just glad to be away from the zombies. And even happier to be back with Kez.

I asked him to bring me closer to him under the water. I hugged his large body as best I could and he wrapped me up in his tentacles to keep me warm from the freezing water.

I kissed him underneath one of his large eyes and then he raised me skyward.

I broke the surface like a mermaid and landed gracefully on the deck. I had gotten a lot of practice doing acrobatics with

Kez, so was very used to quick water exits.

Jess and Casey were already on the boat. They hugged each other, shivering and dripping wet.

Kez grabbed them, brought them over to me, and wrapped all three of us in a tentacle cocoon.

Ooo, I could feel the warmth spread through my entire body. It felt so good.

Another of his tentacles snaked into the wheelhouse and piloted the boat away from the haunted house of zombies. He was so multi-talented and picked up on everything I had taught him so quickly.

He had us so tightly snuggled together none of us could move. Not that we wanted to. It was so comfy I could have slept like this for days.

"Oh man, this feels so good," Casey cooed.

Jess murmured her contented agreement. "Kione, could you tell Kez thanks for saving us."

"Oh yeah, he was awesome!" Casey added.

I asked Kez to slip inside me. His tentacles shifted momentarily to let another one enter between my legs. I sighed blissfully. I loved having him in my pussy. It just felt right to have him be part of me.

"Kez, Jess and Casey really appreciate you saving them. And so do I. You're always there when I need you. I love you so much sweetie."

I kissed the side of his nearest tentacle.

"Awww," Casey commented. And I could tell from the way Jess was looking at us that she was also moved by my display of affection.

Kez throbbed inside me and I gasped in delight. "He... says he was happy to help. And... a bunch of personal stuff to me."

"Ooo," Casey chirped. "Tell us what he said."

"Casey!" I scolded, sounding like Jess. "It's personal."

"C'mon Kione," Jess interjected. "We've seen each other naked, cum all over each other, and fought zombies together. I think you can share this with us.

"Oh Jess, you old romantic," Casey said cheerfully as she kissed her girlfriend lovingly.

Okay, I guess they had a point. I asked Kez if it was okay if I told them. He was cool with it.

"He said he loves me more than every drop of water in all the oceans and… that I'm the most amazing creature he's ever met."

I blushed, a little embarrassed at sharing that. But also ridiculously grateful that Kez loved me so much.

"Oh my God, that's so sweet!" Casey cried.

She kissed Jess again, and they made out for a while, turned on by my romance with Kez. Which gave Kez and me time to do some French kissing of our own. He slipped a tiny tendril in my mouth and I gratefully twirled my tongue around it, thrilled to be kissing him.

After our wonderful smooch sessions, Kez asked if we were able to find the antidote, which I relayed to the girls.

"Oh yeah!" Casey answered. "It's up Jess's super-cute butt!"

"Casey!" Jess was back to embarrassed scolding mode.

"Well, it is."

"Um, actually it isn't."

"What?!"

"I… don't feel it in there."

"Let me check. Kez, can you free my one hand for a minute."

I told Kez her request and he loosened his grip on her left arm.

"Casey, you don't need to… ohhhhh!"

I knew that meant Casey had stuck her sexy finger up Jess's even sexier ass.

"Hmm, you're right, it's not there."

"I told you that!"

"I know, but I just like fingering your hot ass."

Jess rolled her eyes. "Okay, fine you can keep finger fucking me, but that doesn't help us with the antidote."

"Did it fall out when we were trying to fight off the zombies?" I asked.

"No, I had it then. I think it slipped out in the water."

"Oh. Shit." I knew we'd never find it if it was in the bay.

"Oh God. Jess we're going to be sex zombies for the rest of our lives, aren't we?"

Jess kissed her. "No sweetie. We'll figure something out. I promise."

Kez communicated something urgently to me.

"Wait? Kez, really?"

I got an affirmative reply.

"Wow."

Jess was studying me. "What is it?"

"So, this might sound strange… but Kez thinks his cum can cure you guys."

The both gaped at me.

"Um, what?" Jess asked incredulously.

"Um, what she said," Casey stated even more incredulously.

"So Kez's cum is a nutrient. When I first discovered him in this cave, I actually survived off of just, well, drinking his sauce."

They both looked at me intently.

"He says he thinks it will have curative abilities on the human body. It's no guarantee, but it's worth a shot."

"Wow," was all Casey could muster.

"What she said," is what Jess added.

"If you guys aren't comfortable with it, of course don't-"

"Not it's not that," Jess cut me off.

"Yeah, we like fucking zombies," Casey added. "So it's not like we'll mind getting our pussies plundered by sexy tentacles."

"But you and Kez are obviously in love," Jess picked up where Casey left off.

"And we don't want to mess up your awesome relationship," Casey finished.

Man, it was like these two had a telepathic link too. Guess it just showed how loving a relationship they had.

"Oh, well, thanks. That's really sweet of you. But I'm okay with it. I mean it's to save you guys from turning into permanent sex zombies. And, well, we're friends now. I want to help you. And so does Kez. So we're okay with it if you are."

They looked at each other.

"What do you think marshmallow?"

"Well, what if we fuck each other while Kez is also fucking us?"

"Oh good idea! And Kione, Kez needs to fuck you at the same time. That will make us feel better."

"And really turn us on," Jess added.

I half-blushed, half-smiled. And then got a pulse in my pussy, and I knew Kez was totally cool with fucking me while he tried to cure our two new, naked friends.

"Okay," I told them. "We're in."

"Great!" Casey replied. "Let's have a super-sexy lesbian tentacle orgy!"

Jess gave Casey one of her classic looks, but also couldn't resist smiling. Neither could I. And I was already getting wet thinking about what we were all about to do.

Kez throbbed inside me again. "Kez! I'm not asking them that."

"Ask us what?" Casey asked, intrigued.

He throbbed harder. "Ohhh fuck Kez! Okay, okay, I'll ask them."

Both girls looked like they couldn't wait to find out what kinky thing Kez had in mind.

"Um, he wants to know if it's okay if he ties you up and treats you like little sluts like he does to me every day?"

They looked at each other. Then back at me.

"Yes!" they said in unison.

They were definitely girls after my own heart.

I squeezed my pussy around Kez's wonderful tentacle cock. "Okay Kez, you can treat us all like huge sluts."

In my mind, I could feel how excited he was. I couldn't blame him. I was too. I knew we were still committed to each other. But I also knew we both were getting turned on at the thought of seeing Jess and Casey be turned into sex toys and do the sexy moaning they were so good at.

He twisted Jess around and positioned her on the deck on all fours, giving us a great view of that perfect ass of hers.

"Oo, Kez!" Casey said excitedly, seeing her sexy girlfriend's posterior displayed so prominently. "Can you spank her hot ass?"

Kez must have read her mind, maybe literally since he was in such close contact with her, because that's exactly what he did.

"Ahh!" Jess yelped as her sensual bottom was slapped by a slimy tentacle.

"Oh yeah!" Casey cheerleaded. "That's it! Do it harder. She loves being spanked."

"Case... uhhh!" Jess couldn't finish scolding Casey as Kez was too busy scolding her ass.

"Oh Jess, we just said we wanted to be total sex sluts. Just admit you love getting some sexy ass discipline."

Casey was so cheery in the way she said it, I had to giggle.

"Ohhhh!" Jess yelled as Kez gave her a particularly firm slap. "Okay, fine, I love being spanked! Kez, please discipline me like the ass slut I am!"

Kez was definitely up for that challenge, whacking Jess's delectable backside with multiple tendrils.

Jess groaned and moaned in ways that made me and Casey get very turned on. And Jess was obviously getting really into as well as we could see some of her juices begin to run down her thighs.

"Wow Kez, you are an awesome spanker!" Casey told me.

She had barely gotten it out of her mouth when he scooped her up, put her in the same position right next to Jess, and started going to town on her cute butt.

"Ahh! You're supposed to be spanking Jess!"

"Oh shut up and… uhhhh… take it," Jess ordered. "You know you love it too."

"Ow! Okay, fine. But you better massage my sore booty later."

"Deal," Jess agreed as her ass jiggled wonderfully.

Kez was still inside of me and could tell I was enjoying the show. And then he decided I needed to be part of it.

He placed me in front of them, wrapped his tendrils all around me, and shook my booty for them.

"Oh God!" Jess commented seeing my ass shake.

Kez gyrated my hips around and made my ass jiggle all over the place. He was having me perform like a stripper, shaking my ass like nobody's business. I had no control the way he had me tied up. He was making my body move in extremely sensual and slutty ways.

"Oh my God that ass!" Casey cried out as she continued to

get spanked.

"Make her shake it harder!" Jess commanded as she got similar slaps to her butt.

Kez complied, gyrating me so violently it was like ripples of water were flowing through my ass cheeks.

Holy shit! I think I'm going to cum just watching this," Casey yelled from behind me.

I couldn't believe Kez was making me put on a slutty sex show for them. I also couldn't believe how much I liked it. I was getting really turned on being made to exhibit my body in all its sexiness for Jess and Casey and loved hearing how much it was making them wet.

Kez decided I had shaken my ass enough. He tied my arms behind my back and spread my legs out in a full split. He knew I was super-flexible, and he loved putting me in this position.

He spanked me just as hard as the girls, and soon the crisp, morning air was filled with the sounds of our groans and our soft flesh getting slapped by a multitude of sexy tentacles.

After all our asses were very red, he positioned Casey behind Jess. Casey's cock was rock hard and it looked a little more ginormous than it was before, if that was even possible.

Kez tied both girls' arms behind them and kept Jess bent over. He slid Casey forward on her knees so her massive cock penetrated Jess's tender pussy.

"Holy shittt!" Jess proclaimed at having her girlfriend inside her.

"Oh my God! Jess you feel even tighter than before!"

"That's because I think you're even bigger than before!"

"Sorry! This zombie cock has a mind of its own."

"Uhhhh, it's fine sweetie. Just give me everything you have!"

"I think Kez is about to."

And with that, Kez thrust Casey's hips back and forth and made her fuck Jess's completely full pussy. I was always amazed at how dexterous Kez was with his tentacles. It seemed he could do virtually anything with them.

He slammed Jess backwards as he rammed Casey forward, spearing Jess as hard as possible. Both women made the cutest and sexiest noises I had ever heard. Well, outside of when Kez completely dominated me and made me utter similar sounds.

He picked up on what I was thinking and placed one of his big tentacles underneath me. He had me facing the girls now, so I could get turned on by how he was fucking them, and still had my legs in a full split.

Then he plunged me downward onto his massive cock.

"Ohhhhh fuuuuck!" I screamed.

He raised me up and down with my legs fully spread out to the sides. It let him get so deep inside me I thought I might explode. He went harder at sensing how much I loved it, making me tits bounce like crazy.

I looked down and saw him slide two smaller tendrils into both Jess and Casey's ass. Both women's bodies tensed up and they groaned sensually.

He kept having Casey plunder Jess's pussy while he pillaged both their tight asses.

And then he was up my ass, burrowing deep inside my anal cavern, and plunging into both holes simultaneously. As I was about to groan in pure pleasure, another of his tentacles found its way into my mouth. It wasn't the one I usually made out with. This one was bigger and was clearly intended to fuck my mouth.

He grabbed my hair with yet another tendril and moved my head back and forth, making me give him a salty blowjob.

I had no problem with that. I had sucked him off plenty of times over the past couple of weeks. I loved the taste of his sauce, and it was filled with nutritious vitamins or something that was good for humans. He also knew it really made me crazy lustful when he filled all three of my holes at once.

I groaned through his tasty cock as my lower orifices got rammed.

I saw the girls were also taking him in their mouths. He moved their heads back and forth as they opened up wide to take as much of him as they could.

I felt a twinge of jealousy at seeing him fucking them in the intimate ways he had only fucked me before. But I knew he had to fill them with as much of his cum as possible to cure them. And as soon as I thought that, I felt him in my mind telling me I was the one he loved. He didn't want to be with anyone else and he'd stop fucking them if I wanted.

I really appreciated the sentiment, but I told him he needed to keep going. Jess and Casey were our friends, and they needed our help desperately. So I could share him for a little bit.

I also realized I had forgotten to tell him I ass fucked Jess back in the haunted house. That was one thing good about the mental bond we shared. I could communicate all this to him while still getting my mouth, ass, and pussy fucked.

I was grateful he understood why I finger fucked her. He was even cool with me fucking them as part of our huge orgy. Wow. What an understanding tentacle boyfriend.

After our heart-to-heart, he got back to work in earnest, fucking all three of us super-hard.

Casey started to unload her epic zombie cum inside Jess. Kez yanked her out and she shot it over Jess's back and ass. He figured the jizz from Casey's cock was making Jess more and more obsessed with sex, so she didn't need any more of that.

He slipped a big tentacle inside Jess's pussy, and I could

feel through my connection with him that he was ejaculating into all their orifices at once. I realized I actually had a connection to Jess and Casey too. Because Kez was so deeply inside so many parts of us, he must be forming a conduit between all of us. That was pretty freaking cool.

I could feel the girls' intense euphoria at having tentacle cum shoot into their mouths, asses, and Jess's pussy all at once. And at their own orgasms that made them squirt their juices everywhere.

They greedily drank Kez's seed, loving the taste of it and squirming their bottoms around as he kept filling their tight holes with liquid, trying to flush the zombie cum out of them.

And then it was my turn. I felt all of Kez's tentacles seize up inside me and knew he was about to unload a torrent of his savory sauce inside me.

He timed it perfectly with my own orgasms. Being connected telepathically really helped us take our sex to a whole new level.

My entire body spasmed out of control as I felt his sweet liquid engulf me. It was a weird but extremely pleasurable sensation to have it flowing into my pussy and ass at the same time it was traveling down my throat.

My own juices were struggling to get out around his massive cock, so they wound up spurting in every direction possible and really soaking my legs and thighs.

He took his cock out of my mouth and placed me on my knees. He held it just above me, and I opened my mouth, sticking my tongue out. I let him dribble his post-cum into my mouth. I was eager to drink up every last drop of him.

He took his tendrils out of my ass and pussy and made sure to squirt the remaining cum over my tits, coating them in his creamy sauce. He was very thorough in making me his slut in every way possible.

I saw the girls were laying on top of each other, exhausted, and they also had some of his post-cum on their backs and asses.

He deposited me on top of them and covered us with his tentacles to make sure we were warm. After all those sexual exertions, I don't think the cool air was bothering any of us.

We lay in a naked heap, all trying to catch our breath.

"How… how do you guys feel?" I asked.

"Full of tentacle cum," Casey replied.

I rolled my eyes. "I meant has the zombie jizz effects worn off?"

"Yeah, I… I think somewhat," Jess replied more seriously. "I mean I still have a burning desire to have my pussy and ass filled, but it's not quite as intense as it was."

"Oh that's good!" Casey commented.

"Um, Case?"

"Yeah marshmallow?"

"I don't think you have a dick anymore. I don't feel it pressing against my ass."

"What?!"

Casey raised herself up, knocking me off her but Kez had tentacles ready to cushion me.

She looked down. Yup, her adorable pussy was back.

She kissed her fingers and then patted her crotch and ran her hands all over her lower lips.

"Yes! My cute little pussy! I love you so much. Yes I do!"

Jess got up too and stared at her. "Case, are you talking to your pussy?"

"Um, yeah. Why, is that weird?"

"Not any weirder than usual for you."

"Hey!" Casey said as she shoved Jess playfully.

Jess caught her and pulled her into a kiss.

"I'm really glad your pussy's back too."

"But I'm still horny as hell too. I don't think all the zombie effects have worn off."

"Well you know what that means," Jess said with a gleam in her eye.

Casey hopped up and down on her knees. "More intense tentacle fucking?"

They both looked at me and Kez.

Kez entered me and let me know he was up for it.

"Let's do it," I told them.

Kez really had his way with us.

He started us off side by side on our hands and knees, our asses touching. As he probed deliciously into all six of our holes.

We moaned and screamed as he bound our wrists behind us, put our heads on the deck, and made us take every inch of him that we could. It was like Jess, Casey, and I were in an all girl a cappella group that specialized in orgasmic harmonizing.

After he shot his loads into our tight holes, I found myself on my back on a bed of tentacles, my legs spread wide by Kez, and Jess and Casey on their knees, their mouths in front of my pussy.

Before I knew it, they were gladly eating me out.

"Oh my God!" I screamed at having two lovely female tongues inside me.

They worked extremely well in tandem, their tongues touching together inside me and then parting ways to explore the depths of my center. Other times one was inside me while the other attacked my clit. Or they flicked their tongues up both sides of my lips to tease me, then plunged back inside my core to taste my womanhood.

I had never experienced two girls going down on me at the same time before. It was wonderful. And it was even better with Kez sliding into my ass and entering my throat again.

As I lay back, overwhelmed by the two tentacles and two tongues fucking me, I could sense Jess and Casey again. I felt them get large tenta-cocks in their pussies and smaller ones in their asses. They groaned and whimpered into my crotch as Kez fucked them mercilessly.

It seemed to inspire them to work even harder at pleasuring me.

You're an Egyptian goddess! Casey exalted in my thoughts.

We worship your pussy! Jess proclaimed.

Oh man. Talk about making a girl feel good about herself.

Kez inquired if I was really a deity among humans. He said he could easily believe I was. That was one of the nicest things anyone had said about me. I tried to explain to him, inbetween all the moaning and shrieking I was doing, that the girls were just getting really into the sex and that I wasn't really a goddess. But I was okay if he wanted to call me that sometimes. And that I wouldn't mind being a Goddess of Submissive Sex for him. He liked that idea a lot.

He also suggested I pretend to be a goddess right now and have the girls service me as my servants. That idea was really turning me on.

I liked that we could communicate mentally through Kez. It would have been hard to talk with a big cock in my mouth. And also challenging for them with their tongues buried in my pussy.

Yes, I am your goddess, I told them. *You must pleasure me until I cum all over your faces and lap up all my royal nectar. And beg my tentacle lover Kez to fill your holes until you can't take it anymore.*

Oh wow. I didn't know I could get that kinky giving orders. It felt kind of good.

Yes goddess, we want the tentacles so bad! Casey replied like a good servant.

Please cum all over us and make us your royal sex toys, Jess added.

Okay, this was so fucking cool. I didn't know if it was the zombie jizz still in their system that was making them say that or just that they loved being submissive sluts. Either way, it was driving me wild.

I communicated to Kez to grab their hair with his tendrils and force them deeper into my pussy. He gladly did so, happy we were working in tandem to show these two how to be good little whores.

My insides felt completely on fire from what the girls and Kez were doing to me. I would have bucked and thrashed like crazy if Kez wasn't keeping me mostly in place with his soft arms.

Jess and Casey gave me the most incredible oral sex I had ever experienced. My cum erupted out of me, splattering both their faces. Kez moved my hips around and smashed their faces into me to make sure they were completely covered in my juices.

At the same time he exploded into my ass, my mouth, and both of the girls' pussies and asses.

And I kept cumming. No matter how much I soaked them, my two nymphtastic servants kept lapping up my girl cum like it was the tastiest substance on earth. Fuck that was so hot.

I thought Kez might be done with us after that, but I was totally wrong. He dropped the boat's anchor and then lifted us all over the water, twisting us in various ultra-submissive positions and inserting even larger tenta-cocks in our holes.

Guess I wasn't the goddess anymore. He was back in charge. I was okay with that. I could always play a sexy deity again later.

A cacophony of our sexy siren calls carried over the water. Hopefully, the zombies on land were enjoying it.

We were all suspended near each other, with tentacles

inserted everywhere possible, and perfectly plundered by Kez.

He moved Jess and Casey into each other, intertwining their limbs and freeing their mouths so they could kiss each other.

Their mouths met ravenously as Kez continued his exploration of their other holes. I could feel through our connection how much they loved each other, how they were both afraid of losing each other with all the zombie nonsense going on.

I smiled internally, feeling the warmth of their relationship.

Kez brought me a little ways away from them so we could have some kind of alone time. He pulled out of my mouth and I hugged that tentacle fiercely.

"I love you Kez. So much."

I could feel him throb inside my pussy and ass and felt almost overwhelming love and tenderness in reply.

I hugged him tighter and then took his tendril back in my mouth, wanting very much to make love to him.

I gave myself over to him, letting him have complete control of my body. I trusted him completely.

I felt a gentle breeze over my naked body as he moved in and out of me gently, making sweet, passionate love to me.

I made out with him the entire time. I felt totally at one with him as my tongue melded with his tendril, as his tentacles filled me with delight, and as his other arms surrounded and caressed my body.

When he came inside me this time, it was soft and gentle. I squeezed him with my pussy and ass, wanting to milk all his loving seed out of him and make it part of me. The more he was inside me, the more I felt connected to him. It was a connection I never wanted to lose.

I could sense that Jess and Casey were orgasming as Kez filled them with more of his sperm. And they were still kissing, locked in a loving embrace.

When we were finally done, he placed us gently back on the deck. I could sense that Jess and Casey were cured of their sex zombieness and were eternally grateful to us. And that they needed to sleep for a very long time.

Kez and I retrieved pillows and blankets from the cabin and made a makeshift bed for them on the deck. Jess wrapped Casey up like a pretzel as they lay on their sides and Kez tucked them in.

I heard them murmur gentle love notes to each other just before they drifted off to sleep.

Kez created a bed of tentacles for me nearby and I settled into his warmth. He wrapped his arms all around me and nestled comfortably inside my pussy.

I looked over at Jess and Casey, looking so peaceful and cute together as they slept. First a tentacle creature, then zombies. What was I going to run into next?

I felt Kez inside me.

"You're right. Whatever is it, we'll face it together."

I wrapped my arms around his nearest tentacle and closed my eyes as he surrounded me with his warmth.

I couldn't wait for our next adventure.

Thank you so much for reading Tentacle Submission! I hope you enjoyed Kione and Kez's sexy adventures with Jess and Casey!

Check out Jess and Casey's first adventure with zombies in Lust Hunters: Wicked Desire - Now Available on Amazon!

Sign up for my **E-Mail List** at RileyRoseErotica.com and get a **free eBook!**

Please Follow Me on my Amazon Page so you can be alerted to all of my new books and see all my current stories in publication.

Check Out My Other Fun and Sexy Books - All Available on Amazon!

The Mara and KATT Sex Chronicles
Mara Keoni is a sexy Navajo special agent of the Independent Justice Foundation. But she never expected to be paired with KATT, an incredibly advanced female AI inside a sports car. Not only is KATT very eager to help Mara on her missions, but she's also eager to pleasure Mara in every way possible with her many "enhancements." Will Mara succumb to her curiosity and find out exactly what KATT can do to her? Find out in Submitting to My Robot Car and Seduced by My Robot Car - Books 1 and 2 of The Mara and KATT Sex Chronicles!

Laia Rios: Sex Raider Series
Laia Rios is the most amazing adventurer and relic hunter on the planet. When she gets word of a new clue to the legendary Lust Idol of the Amazons, she can't pass up the opportunity to find it. And all she'll have to do is pass through a temple filled

with the most elaborate sex traps ever and submit her body to a bunch of Amazons with the most amazing bodies on the planet. Will Laia be able to withstand all the Amazons' physical and sexual tests? Find out if the Sex Raider is up for the challenge in this sexy and fun action/adventure erotic series!

Submitting to My Neighbor the Witch

Elena Cortez loves Halloween. So when her new sexy neighbor Cassia invites her to a Halloween party, she's super-stoked! Only problem: Elena thinks Cassia might be a witch. Like a real witch. Who's using her magic to make Elena have the most epic orgasms of her life! Will Elena be able to discover the truth about Cassia? Will she let herself become the ultimate witch slut? And will she let Cassia put her wand wherever she wants? Find out in this fun, Halloween-themed erotica!

Demon Hunter Ashlyn: Sexy Demon Hunter Series

Ashlyn Summersnow is a sexy Half-Elf who loves hunting Demons. She just happens to have a penchant for losing her clothes while she does it. Ashlyn is on the trail of Thalia, a sneaky succubus who's having sex with everyone. But will Ashlyn be able to dispatch the most beautiful creature she's ever seen? Or will she succumb to the succubus's sexy wiles and let her do naughty things with her tail? Find out in the Sexy Demon Hunter Series!

Visit RileyRoseErotica.com to learn more about my books and the Decadent Fantasy Universe!

E-mail me at Riley@RileyRoseErotica.com. I would love to hear from you!

Check Out My Sexy/Geeky Social Media Links!

Facebook.com/RileyRoseErotica

@RileyRosErotica on Twitter

@RileyRoseErotica on Instagram

About the Author

Riley Rose loves writing fun and adventurous erotic fiction set in the action and fantasy genres, focusing on stories with heart, humor, and characters who keep losing their clothes. Riley is working on a shared universe of erotica, the Decadent Fantasy Universe, where characters from different series and stories will crossover with each other. Blending action, humor, and sexy shenanigans, Riley brings a unique blend of sweet and sexy stories featuring fun-loving characters, whose adventures you'll hopefully want to follow for a long time. Find out more at RileyRoseErotica.com.

Printed in Great Britain
by Amazon

76524671R00047